SEODA
1 3 5 9

E'NGI - THE REGENERATION

Book
ONE

genevieve arisen

Editing / Book Layout by
Passionate Words Editing Services

DEDICATION

This book is dedicated to
Glen & Josh
and
those who helped me walk my path

"Yesterday you were creating the path
Today you are walking the path
Tomorrow you are the path."

Rev. Dr. Marie Brevil

CONTENTS

HISTORIOGRAPHY OF SEODA 1359

Seoda1359 is loosely based on the island of Barbados, located 13°N 59°W. The rich history, mystery, legacy and people have inspired a new time and space, leading to my writing the story of The Regeneration of Seodans in the genre of Hi-Sci, (History and Sci-Fi).

MAIN CHARACTERS

Nav'aeve (Nah-ah-veev) a Kro'nokai — has control of The Regeneration.

Ryel (Rye-el) is her adopted grandfather — a Viden — his visions are coming true; he is also Nav'aeve's guide.

Ryleba (Rye-lee-ba) is Ryel's sister - a Mkunga, a birth helper.

Diverse languages, numerological theories, science fiction and mythologies were used as inspiration to imagine the world of Seoda1359.

Now it is up to you, fellow creative, to join the Regeneration through your imagination.

THE VÈVÈ OF NAV'AEVE

THE BEGINNING

"Wait, Granfadda, yuh know wuh gine on?"

Nav'aeve was hollerin' down the passageway of his house, her voice echoing off the coral stone walls as she rushed into the main room towards her grandfather, her purple-hued skin complimenting her long mulberry coloured locs, which were skipping along with the excitement she exuded, her radiance exploding into *13Conchshells,* the name of her grandfather's chattel home.

Ryel, startled at her sudden appearance and loud voice penetrating his quiet-time, looked at Nav'aeve longer than usual.

"This girl turns up at some weird times," he quietly muttered to himself.

"But nevertheless…" he sighed, offering her greetings as he got up from his day-bed, which was placed in just the right spot under a calabash tree, its evergreen leaves shading him from the day-high light.

His guards went on high alert at her sudden appearance, but he dismissed their concerns with a wave of his hands.

"Get used to her doing that. Keep her aura locked into the portals so you won't have to always be so edgy," Ryel conveyed to the Ganaim.

"Hail, Kro'nokai Majestri."

"Hail, Viden Majestri, Grandfadda Ryel."

She completed the greeting with the customary dip of the head, right hand at her side and outstretched left hand, palm up as expected when greeting an elder or ancient Majestri.

He, in turn, reached out his right hand, palm up, with his left hand behind his back, as a sign of reverence towards a younger Majestri.

To complete the greeting ritual, they reached for each other's forearm, locking their outstretched arms to invoke the rites of peace to each other.

"I speak peace to you and your home, let mercy, grace and favour be with you always." The ritual was completed by unlocking the forearm, so a single handshake concluded the greeting.

Elder Majestris tend to seal the ritual with a hug.

The presence of Nav'aeve during his quiet-time meant she had downloaded a message, and for her to take the time to teleport to him meant the exciting news was burning her nerves to keep it a second longer; she just couldn't keep it till a Majestri meeting. He also knew it was her respect for him that allowed her to travel outside the protection of the guardians he assigned to her, just to speak directly to him.

"I sure the guards think she is still inside her home," he quietly giggled at the trick she pulled while marvelling at how their telltale purple skin struck a stark contrast to the white interior of his dwelling, a reminder of bloodline powers.

Her hue was just a little different to his, but it still carried the tell-tale purple that told of her heritage. As Ryel continued to look at his new granddaughter for a tick longer, he comprehended the deep sorrow he felt as he thought of her life and role, of how heavy a responsibility she will carry, but, while her skin showed her heritage, it would always be a sore point to others who didn't see what he saw in her.

The rhodolite soil of the land gave Seodans their variety of hues, but the E'ngi power and the purpled skin was an honour to bear as a Majestri.

SEODA 1359: E'NGI – THE REGENERATION

In Seoda1359, Majestris were eminent advisors and seers on government, military, religious, educational and spiritual issues, their endowed power — called E'ngi — was gained primarily through heritage, but each Majestri had to be trained according to their E'ngi.

Few Majestris possessed more than one E'ngi, and those who do were given the title of KaMajestri. Ryel was a KaMajestri, making his eminence in Seoda1359 equal to a Prime Governor. After training, a Majestri lived in service to the interplanetary system they lived in.

The sovereigns of Seoda1359, Seodans, had a curious but revered fear of the Majestri, yet, a regular source of resistance of their impact came from the Ecclesia, who governed the spiritual paths, and who regularly sought to intervene in the work and influence of the Majestri over Seodans (albeit with little to no success in their ranting and objections), and the Legislative councils, since they believed that they had too much power. But they persisted, nevertheless.

Majestri channelled messages through the Mu'vix, the controllers of the atmospheres, who communicated the messages directly to Seodans. They also transmitted into further systems and intergalactic worlds acting as conduits for Majestris living outside Seoda1359. Mu'vix also opened portals to other galaxies to ensure commerce and everydayness was completed. Yes indeed, Seoda1359 is a magical system and Nav'aeve was in the right frame of time for its change.

The sovereigns of Seoda1359 and the planetary systems had formed a symbiotic relationship that spawned a galactic energy for the protection and continuity of their ways of living. Their love for the land was borne in the affectionate name Seodans called Seoda1359 — A'Seo — a name given by the forefathers but which stayed throughout the phasis of A'Seo. Seodans had a most hilarious way of calling themselves when they joked with others about their heritage and shortened name, "Ah-SeeOh".

Since the advice and guidance of the Majestri was respected and revered, many who needed advice travelled to sit with them, even if was for a flutter of time. Those who visited KaMajestri Viden Ryel sat under the calabash tree, as he enjoyed having moments from the forefathers time in his time.

Few Majestris dared venture outside the land without the protection of the Ganaims — their indigo coloured, bearded protectors, who dwelt under the crystal waters that surrounded A'Seo.

The Ganaims were a guardian sect; many were at least 7 statures high. Their bearded appearance and indigo colour spoke of their origins from the planetary system Rouga. Their nature as guards was known far and wide, and few would dare challenge them, making them a formidable force, all except the Qav, a sneaky bird-like kind of sect whose beguiling nature was used by sects who wanted "special" jobs done. A Qav's ultimate dream job was to take down the Ganaim.

As the Ganaims traversed the seas, they rode a magnificent sea creature, a Zar, which flew above the waters they patrolled, but they also lived in those depths with the Ganaims. The Celestials of A'Seo regularly chased after them as they patrolled in a game of 'Catch the Zar'; they know they will never be able to catch one, but the thrill of chasing after them brought the Celestials much joy. The Zar was a four-winged creature with a beak like an eagle and the grace of a manta ray.

As ships entered the boundaries of A'Seo, the Zar would go out to investigate, then they would return to give a report to the Ganaims, who guided visitors to the various landing ports.

While on land, the Ganaims used a Mwar vessel that allowed them to fly the skies and traverse the land as they patrolled or were transporting a Majestri or a member of the Junta Assembly. Ganaims reproduced their own kind as they sought fit, a process that not even the Ecclesia interrupted.

Nav'aeve's bouncing around without saying a word of the download was getting to him as he snapped out of his idle thoughts.

"No, tell muh," he replied, slightly agitated, because, once again, she had already figured something out and expected him to know at the same time.

"Her psychic abilities seem to come through at the strangest moments," he thought.

"Anyways, wunda wuh she want?"

Ryel accepted the calling, no, hollering, of his newly founded granddaughter, adopted in kind, but a granddaughter by respect.

Her speech was punched with the verbs and nouns that formed a music he did not realise he needed to hear,

as she excitedly unravelled the sequence she downloaded through her Majestri E'ngi power — Kro'nokai,
time-keeping.

Ryel was spending his ancient-time in a greater
peace than that of his youth-time, the memories of battles
and federal work, including ambassadorial assignments,
far behind him, but this quiet-time brought him to the guidance time for his newly adopted granddaughter who was
keeping him on his toes.

Nav'aeve came into his life when some of his visions from many phasis prior were now coming to fruition,
but he knew he didn't have the life cycle to complete
them; indeed, he even accepted that not all were his as-
signment, so he submitted to the Fates when Nav'aeve
showed up, a foreshadow of what was to come.

Nav'aeve's presence made him reminiscent —
even sentimental — of those phasis, but he was equally
thrilled and eager of what time was bringing.

For a Chosen, ancient-time meant that a Majestri
like Ryel chose a younger Majestri to process through
Kuongoza, the guidance walk — where they were instruc-
ted into the role, but also when their E'ngi power was re-
fined.

Instructions included how to display their power and how to perform rituals and rites, but they were also educated about history, politics, social, spiritual and scientific issues. The Ganaims ensured they knew how to battle.

This was all designed to safeguard them as eminent advisors for the Head Table of Juntas — the assemblies of Prime Governors and Legislatives of the Tsewedi system where A'Seo was located. A'Seo was led by Prime Governess Am'eymoi, who was a Polito Majestri. However, Nav'aeve was his Chosen.

Kuongoza began when the young Majestri displayed their E'ngi power to an ancient. On recognition of the E'ngi, the ancient was expected to ensure that the younger Majestri was presented to the Eminent Majestri Assembly for validation. The processes to get there, however, were heavily guarded, as they involved public displays of the power and meetings with the Juntas.

A Chosen was required to be of the bloodline, energy and character of the Majestri to qualify for authority in the land. They were usually selected from their youthtime and placed in training, but sometimes, a young Majestri escaped the call due to their upbringing, like in Nav'aeve's case.

SEODA 1359: E'NGI — THE REGENERATION

She was the daughter of a servant at the house of a Numerus Majestri, one who was so adept at the manipulation of numbers he played with them backwards for the fun of it. The servant's daughter caught the eye of his grand-celestial; Nav'aeve was the result.

Due to her conception being through the servant sect, who was not of special heritage, she was rejected as being important to the future of Seoda1359.

Nav'aeve, however, chose to come to Ryel from among the many elders and ancients she met, since his visions were similar to hers. She listened to his speeches and, when given the opportunity to meet him, he immediately knew the force she carried, even though her tell-tale skin stood out.

He met her at the Convention of Sacred Elders, which was mandated by Prime Governess Am'eymoi, as an attempt by her to keep the purpose of the Majestri and Gatherers in the minds of the Seodans, since their power kept A'Seo from fully replicating the Subjugation as they daily lived. A task that was growing harder to maintain as each phasi of time moved. Some Seodans even welcomed the Subjugation and saw the Way as being a great burden to bear.

Even though Ryel knew her power to be that of a Kro'nokai, he was cautious. In his soul he knew, yet he could tell that she did not know her full E'ngi.

However, since she was rejected due to her heritage, she was in the deep, soul cleansing ritual of *novema*, which must be administered first before her full transition into becoming a Keeper of Time.

Novema will assist her in facing wounds of rejection, abuse and ridicule borne since she came into waken-life. The process involved deep consulting moments with Priestess Mrei, who was versed in the novema. Going through it made her sometimes question whether she was good enough or if she had made any progress in her healing or life. Nav'aeve wallowed in self-pity daily.

Priestess Mrei sought to administer the process of self-compassion, something that Nav'aeve needed as she was battling a deep emotion that was refusing to let go. The emotion seemed to sit in her core and wove itself into her very aura.

Priestess Mrei told her to not dwell in self-pity anymore by feeling and embracing the joy of self-compassion on a daily basis, and to look at how harsh she was to herself, hindering how she loved the child who was rejected.

Nav'aeve was reminded that she was to make herself a priority given her coming role, when she would have to silence a lot of voices, especially those who would seem to be on her side but in reality would secretly try to undermine her value.

Nav'aeve learnt how to stand her ground, set tight boundaries and not practice being so harsh on herself. Even though she was to respond compassionately, it didn't mean being so compassionate that she took on the harshness onto herself hindering her own growth.

"Self-compassion is not self-pity, Nav'aeve, and you have wallowed in self-pity for so long you do not know the difference anymore," Priestess Mrei said to her.

To help Nav'aeve absolutely remove the emotion that dwelt in her, she had to embrace a horrible truth: fear and rejection were instilled into her from the moment of conception to waken-life, living in her and dwelling in the same manner as her natural bodily functions. So in the moments of novema where she faced that dark side of herself, Nav'aeve had to process that she would either accept the call of The Sophi awakening her consciousness and her E'ngi, or continue living as a social outcast.

Novema took a phasi to complete.

"Ryleba coming! I saw it as I read the stones by the water.

"She is coming, and she will bring change, but she will also destroy in her wake if she joins with you," Nav'aeve said to Ryel.

Ryel stared at Nav'aeve in both wonder and fear. Ryleba's returning meant nothing good, yet he was excited. A smirk came as he remembered the rumbles of their childhood play.

"How do I prepare for her return?" He mused over the decision, lost away in his thoughts as Nav'aeve's voice faded away the deeper he mulled over her message.

Ryel watched with absolute wonder as his granddaughter looked into the fires she lit in the sand.

The heat and the pattern of the smoke confirmed what she saw in the stones.

"Ryleba had followed him once again, and her return will bring much change," she whispered to no one in particular, but primarily to The Sophi.

She quickly disappeared to Ryel's sacred temple for supplication with the Divine Ones.

"Creators, Kosmos, Orderers of the World, Givers of Times and Patterns, Great Sophi…" and, with a deep breath, Nav'aeve transmitted her thoughts, supplications and entreatments to the Divines.

"I see your message: Ryleba is coming.

"But what does this mean for Seoda1359?

"What does this mean for grandfadda?

"What does this mean for me?

"Is this the time?"

"Are they ready? Am I to ready them?" she agonised over the right questions to ask, searching her inner chambers for the words to say.

Sorrow, fear, excitement all welled into her inner chambers, yet still she remained bowed before the Divines in reverence as she deepened into supplication on the news of Ryleba's return and the impact she will have.

"I offer gratitude for the protection of my loved ones both now and tomorrow as I enter into the times ahead …

"I offer gratitude that those who will seek my life are already dead …

"I offer gratitude that you count me among your Gemma, your precious ones."

"I offer gratitude that in this present vibration, I am in fact no longer hinged or hindered by the past pains I once bore or faced or endured.
"The power I now accept from my Supreme Divines and Creators is already here"

Her form became prostrate as she entered the meditative state necessary for a visit from the Divine Ones.

Her journey was now.

With her supplication over, Nav'aeve left the sacred temple by walking backwards towards the entrance. No one was permitted to turn their back when leaving the temple; to do so was disrespectful.

"Granddaughta, Ryleba has not come to me in over 20 phasis. Why would she come now?" Ryel asked as soon as she returned to continue speaking with him.

SEODA 1359: E'NGI — THE REGENERATION

"What kinda nonsense yuh talking, girl?"

"Grandfadda, yuh memory not like buhfore, 'memba? Ryleba, yuh sista, she comin' fuh a visit. "She coming back tuh A'Seo." Nav'aeve said in Ichga, the native tongue of the forefathers.

"I just know she mean trouble," she mumbled under her breath.

"Ryleba coming," she pressed, insistent. "You good? You ready fuh she?"

As Ryel sat in his verandah at his meditation home in Tinso-cul, a province that was on the ocean side, and his thoughts were of Ryleba, what she truly meant to him, and what her visit meant to Seoda1359.

He found himself reflecting on being the last of their parents' children and Ryleba, the only sister remaining, yet they both were still grieving the loss of their father by the brute of the oceans, lost to sea by Wildwind1955, when she was yet a child.

He remembered how her grief was not hidden from him when she entered Female-hood without the rites of passage that many fathers were expected to participate in with the family, as a celebration that a femininus Celestial had transitioned to femininus youth-time.

Not even he as her brother could have taken his father's place in the ceremony, so their mother placed a hologram of their father, bedecked in their conjoined life regalia, in the room that day. He could still hear her, in a low, melancholy tone, whispering, "Not the same as the real thing."

He will wait for Ryleba's visit, not knowing what she will bring to his urgent attention. "It would have to be critical. Why else is she here?" he thought.

In A'Seo, they held an ancient magica energy. It was a land new to their fore-parents, and Ryel, Ryleba and Nav'aeve took new names to those of their fathers and mothers.

A'Seo was a planet in Tsewedi, a interplanetary system that sat outside of B'raveus, a three moon galaxy, and where those from the true lineage of the nine energies of E'ngi existed in the different lands.

A'Seo was the place of time, having been charted by horologists to exact Longitude1764. They utilised a mechanism called The Watch, which was so powerful that it was a stand-in for the lunars when the weather was horrible.

Majestris operated under a femininus divine energy sphere called The Sophi. The Sophi's known energy charged the atmosphere and was ever present. Many who were not of lineage knew this secret and would copy or emulated the practices of E'ngi, manipulating the energy fields anyway they could.

Those who manipulated the energy sphere did so to read foretellings for those who inquired for the future of businesses, marriages, life decisions, or to seek protection from others who also took advantage of the Sophi, or to speak to those who had transitioned to the Outer Void.

The continued manipulation of the energy sphere was without true lineage, but she did not refuse those who accessed her energy. Even though The Sophi gave them the answers they wanted, many were seeking more and more of her energy and some even thought it a delight to play with the energy just for the fun of it.

The Sophi's power was waning, since more were tapping into her freely given energy without permission, to gain riches or without gratitude and some, with bad intentions, and the agony of being summoned by those outside the true heritage of Gemmas was becoming overwhelming to her.

"A gathering time was coming," The Sophi spoke into the mordial. "Few will be prepared to survive," she transmitted.

The Sophi lived with the understanding that many did not comprehend the brevity of all of her energy, and that it was not to be used for everything.

The given energy would not have sustained times into times and times thereafter. There was a point when it would start to wane and that time was ascending, but true heritage was the path. The Sophi would bring the change necessary. Nav'aeve was the Keeper of that change.

So, with her collective core, she sent a message for the Gathering to come.

"It is Gathering time," The Sophi transmitted to the Void. "I have little choice," she transmitted once more.

"I must protect the Gemmas and their descendants, the Majestri and all those who dwell where I have placed them."

THE SUBJUGATION

On A'Seo, the ocean and earth appeared one and the same; many days there was hardly a distinction between the crystal blue waters surrounding the land and how it gave the sky a reflected appearance of the waters, whether during days-lights or at days-end, when a kaleidoscope of oranges, blues, greens, purples, yellows and whites lit the sky and the land.

Mythical creatures enjoyed the freedom to be themselves, and the waters, necessary for life, came up through the stones and followed many paths back to the ocean, and that cycle provided the energy for Seodans and animals alike.

And it was for that reason that their fore-parents were sent to Seoda1359 by a High Ecclesia Assembly many phasis prior, to prepare for The Regeneration, after countless were forced into The Subjugation by the Council of Paux-els, those who were in charge of The Forgetting.

Even those of true heritage also had to undertake The Subjugation, sometimes from their youth-time.

SEODA 1359: E'NGI — THE REGENERATION

The Subjugation was a ferocious process in the forgetting cycle that took 400 phasis to complete for each system it was placed. Whenever the Council of Paux-els took control of a system, the Subjugation was administered, thereby ensuring the continuity of The Forgetting into times.

The Council of Paux-els had extracted the right to subject its brutality when they won the Noble Battles of Ak'fuan and La'tawo, the battles to have control of times into time. These were considered the greatest battles of all times before and then because it was the end of times, so to speak.

The Council of Paux-els were acknowledged warriors for many phasis before they found themselves in combat with those from Ak'fuan and La'tawo, two planetary systems that each had two moons and were the controllers of times into times, a bestowment of sovereignty given by The Sophi due to their loyalty to the Divines, their land was insulated with the mineral atomic77 to ensure time was kept.

The battles erupted due to the Council of Paux-els not honouring their end in yet another barter matter. They chose to enter dishonesty and thievery into the time as a way to distort The Sophi.

By slowly tricking The Sophi through the use of sleight of movements, she did not notice their intentions until it was too late. The Council of Paux-els took note of the slight kink in her armour, where she could not see the times in between time and therefore missed when they slipped their ill-intentions into the spaces of time.

The Council Paux-els were entering hunger faster than they could control its sting, so the Ak'fuans and La'tawos offered a barter of food for goods, this worked well until the Council saw that it was easier to take and never barter. Their brutality spoke louder each time they came to barter for food, leading to full-scale war.

The battles were so brutal that the souls who died from Ak'fuan and La'tawo did not compare to those who lived. There was in fact no difference, they had lost control of their time into times and times thereafter.

The Council of Paux-els extracted the knowledge of how Ak'fuan and La'tawo controlled time through the brutal application of energy drops to the Kro'nokais and Numerus Majestris.

SEODA 1359: E'NGI — THE REGENERATION

They then took the knowledge to their Judicials of Knowledge to modify the power so it empowered them and weakened whoever was administered with what they then named 'The Subjugation', its hold could now be transmitted through time into times and times.

The Council of Paux-els only saw time as numbers in motion and ignored the advice of the Kro'nokais and Numerus Majestris of Ak'fuan and La'tawo not to play with time and numbers as one and the same, as this would be the grievous error that would spell their doom in times to come.

The Kro'nokais and Numerus Majestris told them that in the four corners of time there was no linear nor perfection in its creativity, as long as there was alignment. They told them that time was the force as the centre of the strong place of energy and balance. Time was the anchor and therefore the stabiliser.

Many Kro'nokais and Numerus Majestris were hidden and sent away for their protection, but on winning the battle, the Council of Paux-els entwined the stipulation that all under their control had to be subjugated, to remove the memory of forefathers and the powers they possessed.

SEODA 1359: E'NGI — THE REGENERATION

Never again did they want a battle of time to be fought by those who had the capacity to win or remember, for time was their weakness and no one was to know.

The Council of Paux-els then lorded their absolute control of the planetary systems for phasis into times. But their intent was sinister beyond the times they stipulated; they wanted more.

They demanded that the Subjugation involve military, religious and spiritual rites, and various educational tactics in different places. Sometimes, however, the rites were combined all in one place instead of being spread.

What the Council of Paux-els did not count on was for The Sophi to keep sending signals and sigmas to those who are of the E'ngi heritage by true lineage. It was that true lineage that allowed reconnection to The Sophi, so they could find their way back to recalling their original power, The Remembrance.

Those who remembered came to A'Seo to prepare the path for others, even if it meant living among those under Subjugation, or sometimes experiencing its effect as well.

SEODA 1359: E'NGI — THE REGENERATION

After remembering, and on completion of the 400 phasis, there were to prepare for the final phase, The Regeneration.

Seoda1359 was also the landing base for the home planet Aki'xeiquxi, some 90000 light years away from the splashes of water which the ancients and elders called, Tumbo — The Womb.

On Aki'xeiquxi, the ones on the land were called Servgens — the night people — and appeared so even in the light of the sun.

The Sevrgens dwelt in the presence of Survres, who appeared as day people, but who also took on various reflections of the daylight. The ones in the waters were called Shebvas, for they connected to the seven oceans, but all were of The Creators and Divines.

THE VISIT

Ryel placed his head down for the night.

Dreams and fairies accompanied him, but the visit of his sister Ryleba he remembered when the sun rose from its night's-rest, since the dreams were just his nerves playing with him.

He smiled at the memory of his sister and eagerly prepared her place in his chattel home.

On the rising of the daylight, Nav'aeve came to Ryel.

"Grandfadda, yuh fussy or wah?" Nav'aeve said, again in Ichga.

"Yuh ent see yuh sista fah suh long," Nav'aeve continued, "Yuh fuhget she!"

In short order, after Nav'aeve said those words, she saw Ryleba barrelling down the dusty road in her starship, spectacularly painted in the latest craze colour of Salem and bright headlights, as it was nights-end. She parked it in front the steps of 13Conchshells and ran to see her last brother.

SEODA 1359: E'NGI — THE REGENERATION

On realising that nights-end had come, Nav'aeve made her way to her chattel home, 5Seas. She sat on a hard stone and waited until 10:19 prima to speak to The Sophi.

"Great Sophi, there are so many changes and energies happening all at once. Ryleba is here, which means you are about to ascend change, and you want us prepared, but the Council of Paux-els are also administering more Subjugation, even onto the Celestials. Why?

"Should I tell them that the Houores has come?" she asked in her inner chambers.

The Houores were the femininus' presence of change, the lineage that Ryleba was a part of. Her living as a Mkunga meant that she came to help bring Celestials into waken-life, but in this case, she was the sister of a Viden, which meant that she was not here to only administrate births but to ensure his visions were protected.

"Can I let them know that you answered me by letting Lī'htan light the eastern sky?"

Lī'htan excitedly struck the sky with an orange glow that melted into a warm yellow.

"Go ahead," he replied, his voice a deep rumble. "Tell them."

The Sophi replied, "Say to those who do acts of betrayal to the Houores, or put a mark on them, tell them, Keeper of Time, say to them, that the Houores will be restored despite their best efforts otherwise." She paused dramatically before continuing.

Lī'htan struck the sky again in agreement.

"And in this moment, I give you the power of the Primordial Night to speak to those who dwell with the Majestri.

"Say to them, that those who have taken my Celestials, making them stumble into the eternal rest while in their youth-time, even though they came into waken-life — that those who have entered darkness into them but call it Light from the Void — say to them that have partook in this vileness, they shall rest peacefully with those little ones eternally, as sure as seven-eight-nine and the little ones come out to play," she added for humour.

"They will be seen and known eternally as an example of horror and they will live in horror.

SEODA 1359: E'NGI — THE REGENERATION

"Say to them that hunted down the blood of those Celestials will now leave this Void into The Frame of Times, where they will be seen and known eternally as an example of horror and they will live in horror.

"Say to them that sought to use fear to gather energy, 'Peace is the Absence of War'. They will be seen and known eternally as an example of horror and they will live in horror.

"Say to those who have used the energy of The Sophi for gains that have time attached to them, say to them that the energy will return to them naught. The power they seek will no longer come, and those that persist, they will be seen and known eternally as an example of horror and they will live in horror.

"Say to them hold the Subjugation into time that their time is naught and its effects are naught."

Nav'aeve was then given the time to speak her own message.

"To those who have hunted and continue to hunt for the lives of those who have E'ngi power, in Seoda1359, A'Seo, in the system of Tsewedi, may those who commit an act of betrayal or marking them or anyone who is related to them, to commit acts of war against them, may those who do such feel the peace of Lightning, Thunder, Rain, Wind, Sun, Nature and the Seven Oceans and times all at once.

"May those who continue to use Seoda1359, A'Seo, in the system of Tsewedi, with no beauty of love, having sent many into the Subjugation, may those who have forced many into the Subjugation before 1661 time of phasis and after 1661 time of phasis, may they feel and know the energy of Judgement, in the form of justice, divine order, truth, law, custom and peace, and may they be reconciled with those who have gone into The Way of Eternal Darkness in the Outer Void, thereafter, as sure as 7,8,9, with naught as their reward."

The message was transmitted to The Sophi, who sent it to the Signals. On her bow to Lī'htan, Nav'aeve saw how much deeper her work would be.

Sleep came swiftly to Nav'aeve, for the energy of The Divines could be draining and she needed her energy to spend the day with Ryleba and Ryel.

At day-dawn, at the sight of Ryleba, Ryel stared in wonder and wept as he embraced her, laughing in joy at the sight of her Salem coloured starship when she pulled up the nights-end prior.

"Come! Come, sit.

"Nav'aeve ensured that we have meat and drink. How long will you be here?"

Ryleba and Ryel spoke into nights-end, all the while, feasting. Nav'aeve soaked up the stories, while also prolonging her aunt's time before sleep-time. Ryleba spoke kindly to her brother's granddaughter.

"Trust me, Majestri, there will be many stories.

"Ah now get hey! As soon as ah land yuh want me come shore!"

And they loudly laughed, because Ichiga so fittingly described the moment.

Three phasis passed since Ryleba's arrival at A'Seo, and she was settled in a place close to the oceans in memory of her father, a place they called Nitsi, a fishing village, where Seodans enjoyed a beautiful life, and Celestials frolicked in the waters without care.

Nitsi was one of the seven calling places for the fish to gather in A'Seo, especially the winged fish that flew above the waters. They made a delicious soup that many enjoyed and were a delicacy served in times of the foreparents.

Ryleba would spend days-end staring at the waters, her heart heavy in contrast to the joy she could have enjoyed had her father not been somewhere at the bottom of the ocean.

By the first phasi of her return, Ryleba had settled enough to make a living in Nitsi as a Mkunga, her memory of her father ever present, but staying close to Ryel, as he was in ancient-time.

Nav'aeve was about to embark on conjoined life to a fisherman named Ro'alph who came from another village, a place called Holep. Holep was at the edge of A'Seo, with jagged rocks blocking boats from venturing into her waters, so men of the village fished from those rocks for their meat and bread.

"Ryel, tell me something, tell me the truth now. What has The Sophi spoken to you about Nav'aeve? I noticed that you consult her on matters. Does she have a path chosen, is she one of the Keepers?"

Ryel looked at Ryleba with curiosity wondering in his mind at the questions Ryleba was asking.

"She saw me speaking to the waters, Ryel, and it did not bother her."

Ryel eased his head in the direction of Ryleba.

"Look, de girl is oneah we, girl, she got de blood," he said.

"Have you told the KaCouncils or the Legislatives as yet?" she asked.

"*No*, Ryleba!" Ryel almost hurled his reply at Ryleba.

"This ain't no council or legislative matter. She ain't hay to send just anyone to the Outer Void, only those she has been given the mandate to deal with, and I ask The Divines to not let anyone send her there either!" His voice started getting louder.

"No one need to know of her presence, just yet!" he said fiercely, conviction in his voice.

"Why not, Ryel?" she screamed back.

"Because she will stop time!" He shouted at the top of his voice, his breathing becoming laboured as he did so. "She will stop time," he repeated.

"If they do anything to harm her…." he said threateningly, pointing his finger at no one in particular. "She is not here for that, yet."

"She is a timekeeper and those who have been hindering her path believe that she cannot see their works."

"In this time with your visit I knew she was going to complete Kuongoza. I just didn't expect it would have been so soon, because of the very challenging path they live."

Kuongoza existed in the former and future of a Chosen's life. Sometimes it began when they are chosen in their womb, some when they reach five, but all must enter Kuongoza, even though it took several phasis to complete.

During that time the Chosen were expected to keep moving through four to five points of life before they were given the rights to enter into the heritage of their ancestry, but only a Chosen one can guide another Chosen through that time of their path.

Kuongoza was awfully hard on some Chosen in their youth, especially the ones born into broken families, and even harder specifically if they hear The Creators call to them as young ones. The paths they must take can break the will of an Unchosen, neither can they prevent the way the path must take, for even the paths that are bent have lessons for a Chosen.

Nav'aeve was settling into conjoined life with Ro'alph and they were finally going to be parents. In the phasis of their union she was happily enjoying the stages and movements of being with a male conjoined.

Life with him, in addition to all the duties she was heavily involved in, brought a perspective to her that she could not have appreciated otherwise. She saw the necessity of a Celestial's protection and her own healing as she progressed through conjoined life.

"I was hardly protected from the horrors of being a rejected Celestial, but I offer gratitude to you Divines for hearing my laments through all the changing phasis of my time," she contemplated.

Nav'aeve was not happy about how her path took, as she further reflected on her life and Kuongoza, while stooping in the birthing water that Ryleba used in the calm area of the ocean for waken-life. The waters were protected by river stones, built by Ro'alph for her aunt as a present when she began making her living as a full time Mkunga.

The memories of five lost Celestials weighed heavily on Nav'aeve, and for a brief pause in time, she heard their vanished voices echoing a chorus of encouragement to their *ti frè,* the little brother they will never meet, but who they told of their gone presence as he grew in Nav'aeve's womb.

As she felt the soon to be wakened Celestial pressing and turning in his path to his waken-life, Nav'aeve first looked anxiously at Ryleba, and then frantically at Ro'alph, her worry rising.

"He knows the path," Ryleba said softly to Nav'aeve.

"Stay in the stooping position and he will find the water."

She exhaled her past hurtings and agonies into the water, releasing the pain of her inner chambers and very soul, for their agony was greater than the joy she was experiencing as she was about to birth her waken-life Celestial.

Ro'alph was ever present, but he also knew better than to cross Ryleba at such a critical time.

From sleep stage to waken-life into the Light, and with her aunt guiding the waken stage, the pain of her past path became evident as she comprehended it all, as a rush of clarity came through the moments of waken-life.

Nav'aeve smiled in acceptance.

"Those chosen cannot always fight against those who want to harm them, because their harm always is rendered powerless once the Chosen accepts their path," she whispered quietly.

Nav'aeve closed her eyes and listened to her heartbeat and the splashes of the birthing water as the male Celestial emerged into the waken-life.

She tightly closed her eyes once again, but with a heavy heart at the choices given to her. "The times are closer," she sighed.

"The waken life was painless, Ryleba," she said off-handedly, "You were right to bring me to the birthing water." While she spoke, Ro'alph offered gratitude to Ryleba.

'What shall you call him?" Ryleba asked, as she wrapped the Celestial and placed him on Nav'aeve's breast.

SEODA 1359: E'NGI — THE REGENERATION

"We shall call the Celestial, Jah'eden, because I sat in the water as I released my pain."

Ro'alph was beaming with pride. In his inner chambers he internalised the overwhelming relief he was experiencing that his supplications to The Sophi and Creators were answered.

He remembered the turmoil Nav'aeve bore each time a Celestial chose to return to the Creators rather than come to waken-life, yet his conjoined one re-entered his bed-chambers after each grief process was completed.

He recalled the moment Jah'eden was conceived. He was convinced it was a night where thunder and lighten bathed A'Seo with their presence, and all Seodans were forced into their homes. One of the lighten strikes illuminated their chambers with a glow, ethereal almost, and she looked at him with that look he could not resist.

As she reached out her hand to stroke his beard, her thumb gently touched his lips. His mouth formed into a kiss on the tip of her thumb, making her breath quicken.

That kiss led to exploration of every crease of her body, especially between her thighs, his tongue exploring the wetness he enjoyed, reaching ever deeper inside of her as her hands caressed his hairless head.

He wanted her.

He needed her.

He needed her taste and her essence on his lips. Her thighs widened in readiness.

He knew he wanted to take her body to the point where he got what he desired — the flow of her essence, all over his face.

"Like a river…"

He wanted her wetness released onto his face, to be bathed in it, his beard to be soaked and dripping from her warmth, leaving him satisfied for the moment he de-sired. He watched her body heaving from the pleasure as he waited till she was ready to have him enter her.

"Are you ready? The night is ours…"

She was holding Jah'eden close when she heard The Creators remind her not to live in the dread of those who terrored or instilled fear in her throughout the phasis of her life. "Their hold on and over you and yours is powerless."

SEODA 1359: E'NGI — THE REGENERATION

Before she looked into the face of her newly awakened Celestial, she was tormented by thoughts of her past. Looking into his sparkling eyes, however, Nav'aeve finally felt peace. Everything will be all right. Jah'eden, you will be a part of The Regeneration.

We will always be under Grace and Mercy.

THE MIDDLE

5:05 dima. Nav'aeve took note of the light sky as she sat with her writing tablet, recording the events of the past seven phasis since Ryleba, her adopted grand-father's sister, visited, and the subsequent events unfolding for all three of them.

She wrote diligently in order to make it easier for grandfather to see into the stars for his visions. Even though they accepted each other as family they were not, yet their paths connected at the appointed time, so Nav'aeve noted it as a pause in the path of both grandfather and herself.

"From 1359 they will fall," Nav'aeve heard in the echo of her consciousness. She recorded it as a sound of the times-to-come.

She sighed and noted it on the tablet. "I have this coming to be a part of, but what exactly, I am not sure… but I note it, Creators, I offer gratitude for your guide note."

Nav'aeve made her living by recording the movements of people and interesting events that affected their way of living, and while they were many like her, she kept interest in the times before when many were bonded on Hawley1636, the place where the Paux-els developed The Subjugation after winning the battles.

But she was also focused on the times ahead and a major shift that was happening in her time, moments she could not ignore because of their similarities to the times before.

Hawley1636 gave Nav'aeve much to journal about for those times ahead.

Hawley1636 was the brutal home base of the Council of Paux-els, whose policy was that anyone who was brought to their base, a task assigned only to the Holanders, had to serve for the rest of their life, unless they had agreed by contract to come as a volunteer worker — a position not as grand as it sounds, as the alternative was being bound in servitude to the administers of The Subjugation.

Anyone not familiar with the daily operations of Hawley1636, could not tell the difference between those being subjugated and those serving the subjugators.

SEODA 1359: E'NGI — THE REGENERATION

Since the Council of Paux-els maintained this law on their home base, a place called N'tirbanika, on Hawley1636 there was no exception to the rule.

N'tirbanika was a world like Nav'aeve and others had only heard of; the people were so different from those Nav'aeve knew, so many stayed out of their way, primarily because of their brutality. Surprisingly, some from there were also fighting against The Subjugation.

In the days of the Councils Paux-els, The Servgens, Survres and Shebvas were brought there because of their connection to The Creators and Divines, in addition to their ability to handle the heat and rot of the place. The Paux-els made light work of conquering that part of the star system.

The star system Tsewedi was enchanted. Its trees, lands and seas not only fed the people, but gave shelter and fun as well. There were creatures that were fifteen leagues high and some that were so small you only saw them when they swarmed together. At days-ends there were flying creatures that huddled together to form patterns in the sky while making a thrilling noise as they moved, their plumage a magnificent potpourri of bright greens, reds and blues. In spite of all this, the true majesty was in the gems along its oceans' floors. Those gems stayed close to the shores; some also found on land, but continued removal could make the ocean lose its majestic aura, even if it took thousands of phasis.

During conquest, a gem was found that others did not have, and that gem made life miserable for those who were sent to extract it. It was bright yellow and shaped like a lump of dirt, and held an energy that allowed ships and atmospheric instruments to work. The Council of Paux-els made full use of it for their system, becoming even more powerful and wealthy However, for others, they used the gems to see into other realms, specifically areas of the realm which had more energy than others. Those who could use it became very wealthy as well, but the influence and power of the Council of Paux-els en-sured that all autonomy remained under their control.

From the moment the Council of Paux-els saw the powers of the gems, they called others from their galaxy — and they came in droves, seeking to make as much fortune as possible.

First came those from the Na'pania realm, day people, called the Fuserts. They worked from the begin-ning of the findings, their backs stained with their blood, drawn from the whippings endured from the Council of Paux-els. The punishing work, toiling to extract the gems, being called to war for the Paux-els, along with little food to feed themselves caused many to die along the way.

'Day people' — an ironic name, because the day people did not do well by the dawn-high light; they were called day people because their skin appeared as an eerie light glow.

The dawn-high light was so bright, its glare scorched eyes that laid bare on sight, and yet the day people toiled for gems untold, using whatever covering they could find to shield their eyes and skin from the glare and heat — but the call of gems made the scorched skin and dimmed eyes worth the pain of it all. Sometimes its draw was greater than the desire to plant and eat food.

The Fuserts dwelt on Seoda1359 for 300 phasis, growing in comfort at the heat and scorch. The soil yield-ing enough to feed the hunger of their stomachs, but the thirst for gems kept them bound to into times even when their descendants became a part of the land.

Eventually, a mandatus was ordained that was to be followed, even unto death, administered by The Ec-clesia of the Council of Paux-els.

SEODA 1359: E'NGI — THE REGENERATION

The mandatus was strict, and was encrypted in places of honour and worship. Anyone who deviated from it was punished harshly to ensure it was taught into time and times. Many tried to keep the ways as strictly as they could, even in the times of changes and descendants.

The mandatus was administrated through the Ord, Obedire, and Occulto paths of the Hoishua holy ones; some were also seen as gods. They created 13 Tjakars, or steps, to attain true observance rites, which were strictly observed without question.

The Ord was the secret sect who, by oath, tended to the business of the land. They made sure they were careful, never anxious, always occupied and they did their work so diligently to ensure that wealth kept going back to The Council of Paux-els.

Obedire was done through the keepings of icono-stasis mosaic, a type of divinity where the worshipping of a sacred one, the Pantocrator, was upheld by those who swore the oath of observance of monastic rule and who met in places called Kirikas. They wore scarlet robes trimmed in jewels.

Occulto was the greatest of the mandatus, for it was the hidden knowledge of times, mysteries, and magic, few could enter into the knowledge, apart from those born into its heritage.

With the passage of time, the descendants and occupiers of Seoda1359 merged in their practices and lives, making true heritage of a new sovereign.

Nav'aeve made a mental note to search for more information on the Hoishua and their impact on the ways that were kept when she received notice from her personal guard Ganaim Qo alerting her that KaMajestri Ryel was present.

THE LEGISLATIVES

"My granddaughter, I greet you."

KaMajestri Ryel was adamant that Nav'aeve undertake the training necessary to take her place among the Juntas and Legislatives. He met with Prime Governess Am'eymoi to discuss and gain her consent for it to happen.

"The Clans will not accept your proposal just like that Ryel," Prime Governess Am'eymoi said firmly.

"You may be an ancient but you cannot insist on pushing this young Majestri into the Legislative arena, and what does she think of it all?" she asked insistently.

KaMajestri Ryel spoke to the Prime Governess Am'eymoi about his visions of times to come and of Nav'aeve's presence and role in those times.

Prime Governess Am'eymoi called an urgent meeting with the Legislatives, Councils, and all manners of governing bodies to discuss what was shared with her.

That meeting caused a major coudeta and disjointedness that many never saw. When the meeting was over, he went to Nav'aeve to brief her and asked her to think on these matters at hand.

Nav'aeve retreated to the waters for 9 rotas seeking answers. It was in one of those rotas that she saw Ryleba approaching her.

"My brother has told me of your dilemma." Ryleba sat in a comfortable position for what she knew would be another long rotas of talking.

"Yes, it is a dilemma, Ryleba. The councils are disjointed about many matters of the land, the Subjugation and what the future of the Celestials would be, and they do not know that in time those decisions of now will have terrible consequences.

"Ryleba, the times to come will not be kind to those who have stolen the councils in this time!"

Ryleba told Nav'aeve that she sat in the council space and watched it unfold but could do nothing, even though she could have stopped it by supporting her brothers, "I chose to stay quiet, less they turn on me and then come for you."

"Aunt Ryleba, they won't get their legislatives whole again! They will scatter themselves into separate legislatives that do nothing for the good of A'Seo," Nav'aeve agonised.

"This is a grievous time at hand and will!"

"Look into the waters, my child, and tell me what you see coming in the times ahead." Ryleba comforted Nav'aeve.

"You said it, that the times ahead will not be kind to them," she continued. "You cannot change the times past, but — can you change the times ahead?"

"I can change the times ahead, Aunt Ryleba, but I do not have all the wisdom and knowledge to do what you are asking of me," Nav'aeve said, agitated.

"Why are you asking me to change the times ahead?

Why didn't you do the same, Aunt Ryleba?"

Nav'aeve's attention was fully on Ryleba. She understood that she wanted answers to the fraction in time with A'Seo's legislatives, but she also was aware of her limitations as this was not her time to deal with, so, with Ryleba probing and poking her to undertake a time not assigned to her, Nav'aeve's anger was growing the more Ryleba prodded.

SEODA 1359: E'NGI — THE REGENERATION

"You saw 1955 wild-winds, you saw how the great winds tore A'Seo apart, you saw the ships being eaten by the monsters of the water, you saw it all, you saw the Legislative's split, so Ryleba, so why are you here telling me about changing the times now, asking this of me?"

Nav'aeve was shouting at Ryleba. She knew the times being asked of her would usher in a new change.

Tears began to fall onto her favourite red robe, but she desired to let her scream sound out so that Ka'Yah, the Comforter of The Sophi, could hear her cry.

"Ka'Yah, Great Comforter, hear! As I look at the times ahead for A'Seo, grant me access to the knowledge and wisdom to handle this moment and the moments in time and times to come!"

A great wind came surrounding Nav'aeve. It was cool, but not cold. The wind lapped around her feet, and, as it ascended, she heard the voice she knew all too well:

"Remember who you are… We are with you…"

The wind moved away, leaving Nav'aeve stunned, but assured.

"Remember who I am," she said to herself. With that, she turned to Ryleba.

"So, why didn't you stop the waters and winds in the time you saw them?

"Tell me now! You suffered loss that time, so why are you now telling me to do what you couldn't?" Ryleba dropped to the water and poured out her laments, while Nav'aeve listened. In her listening, she saw the way forward.

Ryleba's meeting with Nav'aeve was a moment that raised many issues including the laments of her times past, but it also brought much healing and answers they both needed.

Her father was still in her heart after all the phasis of time. 1955 was a terrible wind, yet Ryleba did not forget him, his smile or his rough tone — yet so loving she had him wrapped around her little finger.

Nav'aeve also sensed the laments of one's inner chambers, but, in Ryleba's case, she saw the coming terror she had to prepare her for.

"Rise up from the water!" Nav'aeve stood in command of the moment.

"Rise up and speak on your sorrows of why you lament on the past!"

Ryleba looked towards the sky and spoke — not to Nav'aeve, but to Ka'Yah. "Great Ka'Yah, look at me now in my Elder-time! I do not desire to reach Ancient time with the loss of my father in my heart.

Hear me Ka'Yah, hear me on the times past. When the great winds came to A'Seo, I was in youth-time when my father went to the oceans to feed our family, he gave us meat from the waters, he gave us joy."

Ryleba then turned to Nav'aeve to continue her lament.

"But as the day the great winds came, he went out to ensure that his boat was strong enough to withstand the winds, and I saw, Nav'aeve, I saw the monsters, the Balaenas, that came up from the waters — I saw them grab him and take him to their realm."

"He never turned around, so he did not see me, but I saw him and the terror of his scream has stayed with me all these phasis!

"Do you know, Nav'aeve, what it is like to watch your father be taken by the Balaenas? Do you know how it feels to hear the great winds howl around your ears and you cannot do anything to help?

"Do you? No, you don't. You have come into A'Seo to deal with times to come, but the times past are still here, Nav'aeve.

"They stare at us in our faces and yet we cannot touch them because they are gone.

"How can you know pain? Nav'aeve, you are a Chosen Time Keeper, you are a resurrected one, chosen for divine times.

"You can walk as a divine one and no one will know, so who are you to demand I tell you why I did not stop my father from facing death!

"How dare you, Nav'aeve, how dare you!" She was screaming, her spit escaping as she screamed.

"My brother is losing his memory, and you are here to aid him in his visions, but this, this is my lament, agony and sorrow."

"Do you know why I mostly lament, Nav'aeve?"

Ryleba almost spat out the words.

"I mostly lament because the great winds called my name in their passing!" Ryleba finally felt free from the secret fear held in her inner chambers for many phasis.

"Many heard it cry my name and when my father was gone they all grew pity on me, Has their pity returned my father? NO!" her breathing laboured.

Ryleba broke down in lament and tears, wiping away the sorrow and grief of several phasis, and the moment she grew strong enough to smile, the winds of Ka'Yah came to revive her.

"A'Seo has faced many great winds in times past, especially in the times of the Paux-els." Nav'aeve said.

"The greatest wind was 1780, a force like no other, which ripped many from their life. 1955 was such a creature too," Ryleba chimed in.

"And I lost a lot that day. I know others did too, but my lament is mine and I carried this for all these phasis.

"My brother had a strong determined resolve at the memory of our loss, the irony not lost on him at the significance of a wind calling his sister's name and that transformed his family, and especially his sister's life, along with the many who lost their boats to the ocean's force." Ryleba's sorrow was not lost on Nav'aeve.

Nav'aeve turned her face away from Ryleba and began speaking.

"I ask, not for myself, but for the short time ahead — for a great wind is coming again and it will be carrying your name.

"You have forgotten, my Aunt, that they now name the winds so in times to come they will know which one visited and why.

"Look Ryleba, look at the way the winds shaped A'Seo since 1955, look at the way it took your father and others, look at the way it removed so many boats from those who caught fish for their meat and bread.

"So now, I have to tell you and others of the winds that are coming this time, the winds are coming, and this time the people will be grateful for its destruction, but it will be called 'Ryleba'.

"Look how they have forgotten the ones who came to save this system from great lament, look how they give anyone access to its majesty.

"Look how its legislatives fight and forge methods of corruption to allow themselves to thrive, look how they gather at days-end in cloaks that hide their identity and they roam around untouchable as they wreak havoc on the collective and Celestials, look how the Subjugation has made them into forgetters and they happily enter into moments of pleasure with ill-intenders offering up their dwellings at a drop.

"Look at how they have partaken in the folly of accepting the Subjugation as their life and they repeat it like a mantra to their lives and the descendants, what folly is that… tell me.

"So tell me now Ryleba, why did you not stop 1955 so I will not take the lament of such a decision into the future of the collective: you, my grandfather, and my conjoined?"

It was   as if the atmosphere knew her words before they were said, and Ryleba seemed to have sucked in her breath to exhale words she held within till they hurt.

"I did not stop 1955 because my father told me not to." Ryleba's head bowed in a sorrow not known before, her voice barely a whisper.

"Repeat what you said Ryleba. What do you mean, he 'told you not to'? Are you saying that he sacrificed himself to the great winds?" Nav'aeve asked in a surprised but concerned tone.

"Yes he did. Yes." Ryleba, for the first time, unburdened herself of the torture of her knowing her past and her father's truth.

"You see, while the winds called my name — and many heard them too — they came again in the afterwave of their passing and told me, no — more like threatened that they would return."

"So, he gave himself to them so they would not return for me, that's why he never looked back.

"He meant for his sacrifice to be the last time a Wildwind came to take souls. By sacrificing himself he gave them an energy they have been seeking to transform into the greatest Wildwind in times to come."

"Nav'aeve, a Wildwind destroys because it seeks the soul of a particular Chosen, one who dwells with the moving waters, the oceans and all in it. You forget dear niece, my Father was of Yti sect, those who controlled the movements of the waters, our mother was a Majestri."

"Ryel lives as a KaMajestri, but he also lives knowing that one day he will have to give himself in order to protect his family."

SEODA 1359: E'NGI — THE REGENERATION

"Even though Ryel and I have knowledge of this, we know — we know! — we too must make the same choice."

"It's the cycles of this system, Nav'aeve, its how we live since The Subjugation".

"In times to come, however, should a Wildwind return, I will be more prepared to offer my life to the service of Seoda1.3.5.9, A'Seo, 1.3.5.9".

"Why are you saying it like that Ryleba?" Nav'aeve asked, extremely perplexed.

"I am letting The Sophi know that I have accepted my fate," Ryleba said, surprisingly nonchalant for such an intense moment in time.

THE ASCENDING

Ryel was resting in his favourite place of his chattel home, the verandah, as the cool breeze from the waters was keeping his mind and body calm as he looked back at his travels to B'raveus and D'nalgne lands, places that left him fighting for his freedom and mind, even though he was there in an ambassadorial role from Seoda1359.

B'raveus was the home of the Paicolu people, who were very different in appearance and manner to Ryel. They were the keepers of the mountains, rocks and valleys of their nations. They too had been subjugated by the Paux-els.

D'nalgne was the new home of the descendants of the Paux-els, and they were ruthless about the place in the land, even though they had subjugated other lands to their control.

Ryel was attacked with a weapon to his head on his first travel to B'raveus, so he returned to A'Seo to avoid being killed, as he feared the actions of the those in B'raveus. The land was overran with descendants of Paux-els and they barely tolerated any outsiders.

SEODA 1359: E'NGI — THE REGENERATION

They had full control of the Paicolu people's com-
ings and goings, and visitors to the land — like Ryel —
were greeted with suspicion, so when the weapon was
held against his head after he asked a question about a
building, he knew it would have been better to get back to
A'Seo, but his trip to D'nalgne was where he feared more
than he ever feared and why he ensured he always had a
Ganaim with him for future travels.

While he reminisced on B'raveus, he did not notice
the quiet of his home, nor he didn't think it strange, until
he saw a Qav kidnapper suddenly appear before him.

Jumping up from his day-bed he shouted for
Ganaim Barra, his head guard.

"Come get me, a Qav is here!" he screamed, but
within a flutter of time he understood that one thing was
assured — no matter how much he guarded against
them, they found a way to infiltrate the protection of the
Majestri.

A Medeora quickly entered the room, and injected
him just as rapidly, reaching his neck with such swiftness
he could not react in defence. As he was succumbing to
the sedative he saw Ganaim Barra on the floor, the last
image he had before succumbing to unconsciousness.

SEODA 1359: E'NGI — THE REGENERATION

When he eventually awoke, he found himself entrapped into a system that took control of his mind using a verdict of mentum incarcerare. The Medeora told him it was due to his activism, trying to stop The Subjugation.

"The Council of Paux-els send their greetings," he was told, and nothing more.

Anyone sentenced to mentum incarcerare suffered long sessions of energy drops into their cerebral cortex. These energy drops were done through piercing the back of the neck where a bolt of energy was diffused. When the treatment was to be given, those like Ryel were taken to a silent room so the screams would not penetrate the buildings.

Ryel was in a state of recovering from one of the many drops when he saw a signum — New Majestri, new lands, new times — but he found the signum difficult to comprehend.

He shared the signum with the Medeora, who was torturing him to speak, yet those who administered the drops looked at each other in wonder and confusion.

"How he could have had a signum when the energy was so strong?" a Medeora asked, most curiously, because it was supposed to shut the brain away from thinking or feeling.

"It is coming, and when it gets here you will be sent back to your planets. The novus ordo is coming, regeneration is coming to your politics, economies and worlds, it will cause chaos in your cortems that administer truth, justice, peace, healing and remembrance. You have taken energies and Gemmas from our lands and yet you won't leave."

One of the Medeora of higher rank took an interest in what Ryel was saying and began recording his words for later examination, but Ryel was adamant that he remain in a lucid state to avoid becoming an experiment by the Medeors Vaidyas, who were skilled in taking the body to the point of death but never releasing the mind from pain.

"Please, I am asking … what was I saying … am I dreaming? Am I still in dreams or sleep? Please do not leave me in this state!" Ryel seemed to be begging, but then he switched, immediately getting serious.

"Take me to the sleep place, but better, get me out of here by 4:00 days-end!"

SEODA 1359: E'NGI — THE REGENERATION

The Medeora ran to the administrative offices to tell them of the happenings and they all began making their way to Ryel.

"How are you capable of giving a lucid reaction?"

"Because I am a Viden. I can see visions and among my visions was you releasing me from this."

The lesser medeora began a frantic search for Ryel's records but before he could secure them a senior medical giver, Medeora Colli intercepted him.

"How did you not know you had a Viden here, giving them energy drops? Do you know what could have happened?" the Medeora Colli screamed at the staff. "Why don't you ever look at who we pick up? Hurry, get him out of here, before he has another sigma and sends a signal to the Majestri, or worse — The Sophi!"

"We knew he was of importance, the Qav told us that he was valuable, and we paid happily for him, but we didn't know he was a Viden.

"So what if he sends a signal to the Sophi, E'ngi , Majestri, Ka'Yah, whoever they call on. It does not matter! We have the technology, weapons and land control. What can they do?

SEODA 1359: E'NGI — THE REGENERATION

"We have the Council of Paux-els on our side."

"Stultus cunnus, stupri asinus!" the Medeora Colli cussed, "IF it is sensed that one of the Videns is under heavy energy subjugation, they will send the Excelsior Majestri, The Gatherers! Get him out immediately!"

But it was already too late. The building was experiencing a shaking that made items fall, medical personnel were running to save patients and themselves.

It was the splitting of the steps and deep cracks in the walls that made the senior Medeora Colli and all his staff come to the same reality concurrently: the incarceration of a Viden was a violation of their code. He sent out a signal for help.

The Majestri knew that a signal from Ryel meant that he was under a heavy energy distress. The Mu'vix tried to intercept the signal so they could translate the message to send for the help they would need.

"The energy Subjugation that *A'Seo Ryel* is undergoing is causing our energy readers to overheat, we do not have time to travel there."

"Hasten, call the Gatherers!"

"Gatherer Nine, we need you and eight Gatherers to triangulate the signal of an important Viden, he's on Seoda1359, *A'Seo Ryel*, they are energy dumping him. Hasten, now!

"We have his signal. They are trying to confuse his thoughts and make him give them all his energy. They want to use him as a source of the Majestri energy, but we have begun to intervene."

The Gatherers never worked so hard to bring a Viden out of distress, but, with Ryel, they would be losing an ancient whose wisdom and knowledge was vital to the changes in coming phasis.

The energy the Gatherers emitted became an earthquake where Ryel was held, yet the Gatherers did not stop, they meant to make the Medeoras pay for their insolence.

"Gatherers, do not withhold your energy, our son needs us!" Gatherer Agur screamed at Gatherer Nea.

"Earthquakes are happening, Gatherer Agur. The buildings are shaking and tremors are as far as 6 miles outward; this energy was meant just for their location!"

SEODA 1359: E'NGI — THE REGENERATION

"Get him out NOW, they are destroying the building. Get him OUT!"

The scramble to get Ryel from the medical facility was the fastest all the workers saw, but Ryel knew it would have come. He quietly watched, in the chaos, as the facility did all they could to get him out and at the time requested.

Most Elder Medeora Colli requested an immediate update on the structure of the building and patients, being grateful that any damage was repairable and no deaths occurred, but he knew that another 10 pars and they would be looking at a massive happening that would not only set them back but would bring their city to ruins.

Some 40 phasis later, Ryel sought counsel to hold the Medeora accountable for their decision to administer the energy injections. Counsel for the Medeora was ruthless in their defence, claiming that Ryel was a reprobate and not deserving of any reward for their mistakes; the legal arena was up in arms on both sides.

Ryel did not care about their position and took his petition to the Utmost Judicial of the land. His anger rose when the Medeora sought to betray the trust they were swore to give by losing his information and sending false information to the High Council about his charge to them.

It took 30 phasis later for the Medeora to admit their mistake and see that the decisions made during the incarceration of Ryel could have been avoided if they had consulted their records about who he was in the land, and not be dishonest.

Before the moment of confession, they experienced many strange things in their facility, but even that did not make them confess, until one of their Council forced the case due to his own personal experiences with strange happenings and he knew, even if it was hard to admit.

The Gatherers were defending their Majestri and that defense came in ways that those who offended could not withstand the judgements they faced daily.

TIME TO GATHER

Ryel's rescue allowed the Gatherers to bring him to the Chambers of Healing for 3 phasis. He needed the time to recover from the energy drop of the Medoras, but he also needed the time to share his visions with the Gatherers.

Deliberations and preparations for his return to A'Seo were constantly being discussed at Pagav, the home the Gatherers gave him while he was with them.

The Prime Governess Am'eymoi and Juntas were assured that he would be returned to A'Seo, but not when. That was necessary to avoid him being recaptured, or worse.

The rescue of Ryel forced The Gatherers to prepare to come to Seoda1359 but it also was the time, even if time had forced itself to happen. They would have to dwell in A'Seo until The Sophi told them it was time for them to act.

The Gatherers' presence would be a stark reminder of their power and capability, since A'Seo lost their connection to them over the phasis. The Gatherers sat as the ArcGuardians of Seoda1359, they stayed in ready to be of service to the Divines once pressed into duty in situations like the one with KaMajestri Ryel.

They watched and, when possible, guided a Chosen when the times showed a spark of connectivity. The connection of Nav'aeve to her E'ngi caused the Divines to hasten the Gatherers' sense of alertness.

Their reintroduction had to be done as dramatically as possible to avoid any hindrances or sabotages, especially by the Ecclesia, who was already gaining followers and causing much chaos because of the Medoras' actions.

Gatherer Nine conferenced with Ryel on the moment they would return. He chose the location and convened the message to the Mu'vix.

When the day arrived, many assumed that the Regeneration had begun. The noise, winds, lightens and shakings of their craft caused chaos in A'Seo and their physical presence shocked, startled, rattled and confused many, but as soon as they appeared in A'Seo the streets were filled with the souverigns celebrating the return of the Gatherers, merriment ablaze in villages and cities, but mostly in the hearts of those who were awaiting the judgement of the Council of Paux-els.

"Hasten," Prime Governess Am'eymoi said in the most anxious of ways, "Hasten to prepare a welcome for the Gatherers! They are here, they are here!"

With no time to bring the best of their musicians, dancers and entertainers to have the grandest of parties for the Gatherers, Prime Governess Am'eymoi tried to offer the best that was available for their welcomed presence, so the collectives greeted them with their own singing and dancing, the Celestials' voices out-singing everyone.

Gatherer Nine, the leader, greeted the Prime Governess Am'eymoi to lay out the way forward now they made their presence known.

"We are not here for anyone's agenda, Prime Governess Am'eymoi, we are here for change."

Within the first phasi of their return, and after much conferencing with the Juntas and Legislatives, The Gatherers took over the airwaves to speak to the people.

"When you can take what you have learnt to make it your own, then A'Seo can be free of the Council of Paux-els.

"We are not here for you alone.

SEODA 1359: E'NGI — THE REGENERATION

"We are here to help you, but you must first help yourselves if change must come in the most peaceful, permanent way and The Regeneration is to happen for those broken by Subjugation.

This must begin with you, Seoda1359.

"The time has come, the work has now begun."

When the Gatherers had set their agenda, and had met with Prime Governess Am'eymoi , The Message of The Sophi was received, so they announced the calling forth of the Majestri.

"Prime Governess Am'eymoi , tell the Legislatives to come, we must confer on the changes ahead," Gatherer Nine said.

He paused while putting his index finger on his lips.

"Nav'aeve, she is to be the bearer of the change."

* * *

It was the meeting day for the House of Legislatives for the 33 Segments of A'Seo, all led by Prime Governess Am'eymoi . The Segments identified themselves in four clans, Albo Clan, E'ma Clan, Nydepi Clan and Pa'wah Clan.

SEODA 1359: E'NGI — THE REGENERATION

Despite being forewarned by KaMajestri Ryel, despite meeting previously with Prime Governess Am'eymoi on what would happen for the time they were in, major violence took place in the House of Legislatives.

Nav'aeve was there to record the time, not in her future capacity.   When the meeting was over many rotas later, there was a further fraction among the Legislatives.

Hostility was redirected at Nav'aeve, so she hastened out to avoid being hurt — or worse.

Nav'aeve hastily ran to Ryel to give him the news.

"Grandfadda, Grandfadda, ah bacchanal coudeta in the House of Legislatives!"

"Wah, wuh you suah, granddaugta? Wah you meaning?

"Surely the Legislatives would not pick this moment to break the protocols of the souverigns.

"Tell me what happened, girl, this is a time you did not know about, but you have to journal for the times to come."

"Grandfadda, I was in the House of the Legislatives as they discussed the matters of the souverigns in this time with the Gatherers here. All 33 sector leaders were in summons when a noise came from the back of the room.

"Ten of the Albo Clan motioned to Prime Governess Am'eymoi that they wish to speak outside of the protocols of the matter at hand.

"We are speaking to you frank," they said.

"Wuh she got tuh do wid wuh gine on?

"She's a nobody! Yet that KaMajestri that you keep listening tuh and now de Gatherers pushing she as somebody we all should listen tuh, too … well not us nor we Souverigns. Even the Ecclesia fed up of hearing bout she.

"The Subjugation ain't nuttin to play wid, and a lil frozzi, pissy servant child you want a whole system to follow!" The clan leader shouted.

"We all vote to oust you as leader of A'Seo!"

"Grandfadda, they were shouting, threatening, and then they took over the protocols!

"It was a take-over, a coudeta, and nothing could be done about it!

"Grandfadda, what does this mean for us, for the people of A'Seo?"

"Slow down girl, you are making me dizzy! I cannot think if you are bringing so much information so quickly!" Ryel said, slightly agitated at the news.

"Let's look at the matter at hand, Granddaugta." Ryel was livid.

"This is not a legal decision!" he exclaimed, waving his fist in anger.

"Surely the House of Legislatives and Prime Governess Am'eymoi won't be tekking that as a serious decision of legality!"

Ryel's anger at the matter caused him to shout at no one in particular, but at the situation itself.

"So don't worry, Nav'aeve , the people of A'Seo won't be letting this matter just slide!

"But will this affect the council's ability to rule over themselves and council matters of A'Seo in times to come?" Ryel ask himself.

Turning to Nav'aeve, he saw the fear in her eyes.

"Nothing to fear, Majestri, it just means time is closer than we understood."

"But what if the people are so disconnected from matters that they cannot forge an answer to the goings-on of this time?"

"Remember, Granddaughta, you are here for the times we are in. We are in the chaotic era, the stable era passed many phasis ago, and when a new era arrives the Divines will send beautiful minds to look at the movement of the sun and times, to tell the people of what will be coming and what has passed. The Creators have not forgotten us.

"Do not get distracted my child.

"Look at the times we are in and use the energy of this moment to look into the times to come to see if they will be a pattern of this moment.

"You must decide if the chaotic era that you have been assigned to has the right elements to make it a safe era to stay in for more than 900,000 phasis. This is the time of your call.

"Look and focus, child.

"Look at the passing of the Lights and Nights.

SEODA 1359: E'NGI — THE REGENERATION

"Look at the passing of times and their numbers.

"Look at the connectivity of it all

"Look, granddaughta! Look!"

Nav'aeve took a deep breath and turned to her tablet. Asking of it questions, journaling the times that will forge a new era when the Selene Moon passes in the time of 9000.

"Some questions will be asked of you when time arrives, so pay attention my child," Ryel said tenderly.

Despite the coudeta, the Gatherers forged ahead, dismissing their behaviour as that of Celestials who cannot have their way.

* * *

The day had arrived. The Gatherers were going to announce the changes that were to come.

The people were glued to all types of airwaves. Some surprised, but many more in fear.

At the meeting of the Majestris, for the first time, the Gatherers spoke on the changes. Each was given their task and Nav'aeve was chosen to deliver the message to the people of A'Seo.

SEODA 1359: E'NGI — THE REGENERATION

On the first day of the first vika of the first phasi of the change and the presence of The Gatherers, Nav'aeve presented the message of change to the collective souverigns of Tsewedi. With Ro'alph and Jah'eden at her side, Nav'aeve stepped to the balcony of the Prime Governess Am'eymoi's headquarters and spoke from ancient and prophecy scrolls.

She began with the Woe. The Pronouncement to the Council of Paux-els, their ilk and sympathisers, upkeepers and co-conspirators.

Woe to him that gathereth evil covetousness to his house, that his nest be on high, and guesseth him for to be delivered (out) of the hand of evil.

Vae illi qui congregat malum avaritiam in domum suam, ut nidum suum in altum et nos ut liberemur (e) de manu mali.

After pronouncing the Woe, Nav'aeve announced the Release, a saying from an antiquity forefather from times past.

We have dared to be free. Let us dare to be so by ourselves and for ourselves.

Her voice suddenly changed. It mellowed out, becoming multi-layered. Suddenly, it was as though Lī'htan himself was with her, and as if she became The Sophi herself. As she spoke, he struck the sky in agreement, and all who watched hid their faces from the brightness.

Then she pronounced the Subjection the Council of Paux-els were to face.

For those that designed and placed The Subjugation1661 and its many tentacles onto the sovereigns in times, for times, and times into time, your time in this phasis is now powerless.

Your subjectivity and its works now is powerless.

Your hold over the nucleus of the people now is rendered impotent like rolling stones.

Your voice is now silent.

Your hands are now fingerless.

Your steps are now wordless.

Your Light is now Darken into the Darkness of Dark

Your way's Darkness is now Lit with the Lights of Lights so you will never see your darkness reenter or see its ways into the spaces of time.

Your infractions into the spaces of times are now closed, and those spaces filled with whiteness so that nothing white can be left behind into time and times and into times ahead.

I call upon the dragonflies to seek your works and consume them until your works and fears are finished and have no more presence.

I call upon the butterflies to heal the collectives in the lands that the Subjugation was administered in this time and times into times to come.

Pro his qui designaverunt et collocaverunt The Subjugation1661 et multa tenacula in reges in temporibus, pro temporibus, et temporibus in tempore, tempus tuum in hac phasi nunc impotens est.

Subiectiva tua et opera nunc impotens est.

Tuum nucleum populi nunc impotens redditur sicut lapides volubiles.

Nunc vox tua tacet.

Manus tuae nunc digitus sunt.

Vestigia tua nunc sine verbo sunt.

Lux tua nunc in tenebris tenebrarum obscuratur

Viae tuae Tenebrae nunc Lit cum luminibus luminum ut numquam tenebras tuas reintrare vel vias eius in temporis spatia videbis.

SEODA 1359: E'NGI — THE REGENERATION

Infractiones tuae in spatia temporum nunc clauduntur, et spatia candore repleta, ut nihil album relinquatur

damselflies voco ad opera tua quaerenda et consumenda, donec opera tua et metus finirentur nec amplius praesentiam habeant.

papiliones invoco ad sanandum collectivos in terris, quas subiugatio hoc tempore et temporibus in futura tempora administrabatur

Nav'aeve closed the scrolls. The Litens stilled, and the silence of the collectives was louder than their fears and awe, many of them were in tears that the Subjugation was now over. She turned to the Gatherers and quietly said.

"Gather all necessary far and near. You were forced into our time, making time ascend. The Sophi is waning and cannot tolerate another 1000 phasis, the Paux-els and their ilk must face their judgement."

She spoke to Ryleba and Ryel.

"We must gather all concerned so they will know their time is ascending.

"Gather those who are of Majestri.

"Gather those who are of purpose to The Regeneration.

"I will also call the remaining six energies of the E'ngi into our phasi.

"Their time has ascended.

"Get Seoda1359 prepared for The Regeneration. She said firmly.

"Nav'aeve, how would The Regeneration begin if we have ascended time?" Ryel queried.

His visions were correct, but the timeline was at least another 25 phasis to come.

"The presence of the Gatherers should have been your clue, Majestri Ryel," she shot a look at him that told him he erred in questioning her judgement.

With his hand outstretched and palm up he offered regrets for interjecting at such a critical point. He was terrified because he understood the power she was gently allowing her mind to settle in.

"Because she will stop time," the former conversation with Ryleba echoing in this thoughts. So, with a shudder as he shook off the sudden rush of energy surging in his body, he sank down to a half position of kneeing, due to his aged body and spoke.

"Majestri Kro'nokai Nav'aeve, you are just in your judgement and sight. I am of service to you in this phasi of A'Seo."

"Ryleba!" Nav'aeve almost spat out her name.

"Your time has ascended." Her tone firm, yet commanding.

Ryleba instantly prostrated before Nav'aeve.

"My service to The Regeneration is assured, Majestri Kro'nokai Nav'aeve. I will serve." Ryleba announced.

They conferred on the journeys ahead, each quietly comprehending that they were both witnessing and partaking in the phasi of The Regeneration.

"How far into the future should we consider the consequences of our actions in this phasi?" Ryel asked.

"Should we therefore be thinking about the souverigns in the future?"

Nav'aeve almost hurled her reply to him.

"Using philosophical questions in a moment like this is why the Subjugation was allowed to thrive for times into times and no one had the guts to stop it.

SEODA 1359: E'NGI — THE REGENERATION

"I am not here to debate with anyone, including you, Grandfather. It will not be a days-end of beauty the day I call for death, understand that KaMajestri Ryel.

"We must consider one more factor…

"The Paux-els." Everyone collectively stopped, even their breathing.

"Ganaium Barra. Let not the day-light or days-end fill another phasi and they exist in our system.

"Slay them and their ilk, right down to the descend-ants and those who emphatically side with them.

"Slay their Eccleisla and Mantedus.

"Leave nothing from them behind you.

"Show no fear, even unto the death of your life.

"If you have a moment of mercy, I shall have you strapped to the stones in the day-high light while I light the fire myself.

"Dispatch the dragonflies, and the predators of the air. Command them to eat, command them to destroy their lairs wherever they be found.

"Dispatch the Zars to find their ships and sink them away from our spheres.

SEODA 1359: E'NGI — THE REGENERATION

"Cleanse their Subjugation vessels from our realms.

"Cleanse the atmosphere of their stink.

"Cleanse the realms of their hold on time, times and times ahead."

Majestri Ryel look at his granddaughter with a gleam in his eye. "Novema had completed its cycle," he whispered, in awe.

"She was now in Eminence."

THE REGENERATION

The Regeneration was spoken of in quiet places for 100000 phasis, yet no one believed it would ever be birthed into existence.

The process was addressed by the Juntas and the Governors of the galaxies for 3 phasis to prepare the collectives for the changes ahead. To bring The Regeneration suddenly into the orb field of the collectives would cause absolute chaos and even suicide to countless because the undoing of the Subjugation would strip many away from their comforts, both mentally and spiritually. Regeneration was a full 9 phasi process, so with 6 more phasis to complete, A'Seo was on high alert.

The reality that it came so in-your-face made the atmosphere in A'Seo and the Tsewedi provinces abuzz with anxiety, fear and happiness.

By the 4 phasis of time, Nav'aeve was with Ro'alph and Jah'eden enjoying a moment of celebration prior to her leaving to enter the full transition for The Regeneration when she was alerted by the Ganaims that the Mu'vix were ready to escort her to through the atmospheres to the return, to the beginning of the Subjugation, the starting point necessary to return stronger and better.

SEODA 1359: E'NGI — THE REGENERATION

Bowing low with one knee on the ground and with their right hand outstretched, palm up, the leader, Mu'vix Na'tre, presented her credentials to brief Nav'aeve on what to expect as she entered the atmospheres for the messages they were prepared to transmit as required. The Mu'vix finished the greeting Nav'aeve with a bow of the head but with both hands on their sides.

"Kro'nakai Majestri Nav'aeve, we are of service to you," Mu'vix Na'tre said.

"We have assigned you Mu'vix A'vil, she will coach you on this journey as she is from the ancient times of prophecies and understands the journey ahead for you emotionally.

"She will help you to journey to the parts of The Subjugation that will be hard for you to navigate in your inner chambers as she pulls the Subjugation out of your inner core.

"She's been through times from time into times. Trust her," Mu'vix Na'tre said assuredly.

Mu'vix M'reve gave Nav'aeve her credentials and spoke briefly on the road ahead.

SEODA 1359: E'NGI — THE REGENERATION

Nav'aeve wanted moments to return to Ro'alph's chambers prior to her leaving for her preparation. He assured her that his stance remained the same in these times as the times they conjoined.

Ro'alph saw in her the way he saw himself, someone who was broken but had more inside than the brokenness. He wanted to find a conjoined one who wanted to cast aside the fears, insecurities and pain of being a rejected in the system they lived. He found his conjoined in Nav'aeve.

He was a part of the plan for The Regeneration and he knew that she was critical to its entrance into the times they were in.

He prepared Jah'eden and himself during the phasi he headed the Assemblies of Builders. He was a fisherman, but his skill at building allowed him to build many sites throughout the galaxies. The Regeneration would need spheres to home the spaces needed for healing and growing.

Ro'alph and Jah'eden embraced her once more, surrounding her with their aura. Jah'eden was in youthtime and being tutored by scholars. He whispered to his matriarch.

SEODA 1359: E'NGI — THE REGENERATION

"By the time you return I will be a full scholar and worthy to sit with Juntas." They smiled and did the rites of departure for a long journey.

As she looked on at Jah'eden she recognized his patriarch's looks in his youthful face, his colour a mix of her purple and Ro'alph's rich earthtone, making him a curiously beautiful blend of them both.

"I surely will see more like him soon," she said quietly. The Sophi, ever listening, whispered to her right ear,"Yes, you shall."

Nav'aeve chose to leave A'Seo quietly, she just wanted her close ones with her for such a moment.

Phasis 5 of the preparation saw the call for 144000 of the femininus sovereigns in the galaxies to come be a part of The Regeneration, but the call was not to be jested and many were warned not to answer unless they had undergone nine purification rituals, because if they entered Seoda1359 without the purification administered they would spontaneously combust on contact with its atmosphere, a stipulation put in place by the Mu'vix to ensure that The Sophi was protected in this new dispensation of regeneration.

Taking Ryleba with her, she went into a meeting with Mu'vix M'reve, Mu'vix Na'tre, and Mu'vix A'dul.

The times into time hinged on The Regeneration, but this had been only spoken off for many phasis in times before.

"Tell me, Mu'vix M'reve, how will you administer this phasis.

"Tell me Ryleba how will you administer this phasis."

Nav'aeve held many discussions while she prepared. From the growing of food to security.

Phasis 4 saw the call for 144000 of the masculus sovereigns of the galaxies to come be a part of The Regeneration, but with the call specific in the intent, they had to go under 9 rites of passage which were administered by the Ancients of true heritage in the ways of the femininus. They were also given instructions on matters of family, administration, and business.

Those who answered the call also had to ensure that they undertook the task ahead seriously because they too would burn up on contact with the atmosphere, should they attempt to circumvent the stipulations.

SEODA 1359: E'NGI — THE REGENERATION

By phasis 3 the 288000 chosen were given the choice to conjoin, with the comprehension that they were conjoining for the duration of their existence in the Regeneration. Those who chose not to conjoin were give strict instructions on living as an independent in the Regeneration, if they changed their position to be conjoined they did so understanding that they were conjoined for their existence.

In phasis 3, those in conjoined life were expected to have fulfilled all the requirements for the new tomorrows. The Subjugation was over and its tentacles were cut off from memory, but with the hope for a new way of living, the assurance of those 288000 that they would not have any semblance of subjugation into their teachings or way of living in the tomorrows was sought.

Phasis 2 was also the placing of The Tomorrows as the Regeneration was preparing to launch. The Tomorrows needed leaders in every facet of living from family life to politics and those 288000 were being prepared to be sent into the new atmosphere that the Mu'vix was preparing, the home of The Tomorrows, a place they called A'qlon in the GIRIDIMG Zone, a system that dwelt in the waters above the waters of the atmospheres where the Divine Ones dwelt.

SEODA 1359: E'NGI — THE REGENERATION

Phasis 1 was the launch, the most painful but reassuring of the 9 phasis it took to prepare for A'qlon. The Sophi was transported there from Phasis 9 by the Mu'vix along with those purified who were being sent from A'Seo to assist in The Regeneration, including Ro'alph and Jah'eden, so they could recover and renew their strength while all waited for the 288000's arrival.

Nav'aeve, Ryel and Ryleba convened at 13Conchshell in a moment of sadness as they realized the monumental task they have been administering. The launch of the 288000 to A'qlon was a great day for A'Seo.

On that day the sky was alight in many colours, especially pinks, shades of red and purples. The chosen had already been sent ahead, and those that remained were to be retaught. Nav'aeve stepped into the launch ship. She looked longingly for Grandfadda and Ryleba, knowing they would join her, but still anxious they were not there.

"Are you ready Your Eminence?" she was asked by the Mu'vix.

Nav'aeve was waving to those gathered when Ganaim Barra hurried to the door before it was closed. It was a message from Granfadda.

"Granddaughter, you have been instrumental in The Regeneration, but this journey is not ours to take." She saw that Ryleba had scribbled hearts as a signature and her tears flowed.

Nav'aeve rushed to get off the Mo'iah Starliner Vessel, named for a long forgotten ancient, but the door was already closed and the launch countdown was on. She was heading to The Regeneration without Ryel or Ryleba. This was not how she envisioned the moment when she sat on the stones speaking to The Sophi about the Houores.

This was not what her shouting match with Ryleba meant, this was not the plan, this was not the vision. This was making her panic.

"Are you ready Your Eminence? We will be in orbit to A'qlon.

Please prepare, in 7,8,9..."

All the work Priestess Mrei had done was unravelling as Nav'aeve went into full panic mode, especially as she transitioned through the waters. She felt the weight of their presence. It took her many rotas to comprehend that she was being re-birthed, the launch triggered a long suppressed memory but it finally released its hold as the waters closed and the old system was truly left behind.

Their arrival and settling in A'qlon took another 9 phasis to complete. All the while, back on A'Seo, Majestri Ryel continued to speak to the sovereigns and legislatives on the way forward for A'Seo in The Regeneration they were processing, as their progression was completely different to the 288000 who were all purified and completely removed from the Subjugation.

"They will never have to forget," he thought out loud.

"They and the Celestials to come will regenerate The Remembrance times into times and times to come."

* * *

He smiled as he fully comprehended the brilliance of Nav'aeve's plan as he wrote to her another update of life in A'Seo.

His continued correspondence was a delight to Nav'aeve, especially when they communicated via the tel-coms systems.

SEODA 1359: E'NGI — THE REGENERATION

It was a beautiful star filled moment when her telcoms were signalling more than usual, but he sent her messages instead.

"That's peculiar," she thought, "he never messages."

She sank to the floor of her home with Ro'alph and Jah'eden holding her as she read the message from Grandfather.

"Ro'alph!" she screamed, unable to bear the news.

"Look at this!" she said frantically, tears flowing, as he read aloud the disheartening news from Grandfather Ryel.

"Ryleba is coming, I just wanted you to know. She will be here in 48 rotas.

We are preparing.

The boats are being secured.

My sister is prepared.

The times to come are now here.

My sister is hoping that Ryleba will bring our father's voice once more.

Her winds are too strong to sustain her wrath. Ask The Sophi and Divine ones to send us their grace, but my visions do not allow me to speak another moment of un-truth.

Ryleba is coming, she is a 9. The number of completion and fulfilment."

Ryel closed the note with a quote from a forefather of antiquity times past, the one Nav'aeve quoted for the Release.

"I choose this quote my dear granddaughter, so fitting a quote, I must say, because this moment is the freest, because we have done it by ourselves for ourselves.

"Until…

We have dared to be free.
Let us dare to be so by
ourselves and for ourselves

Jean-Jaques Dessalines."

ABOUT THE AUTHOR

Genevieve Arisen is a family oriented woman. She is a present history student with the University of the West Indies, Cave Hill, Barbados.

Her interest in History and the Spiritual led to the writing of Seoda1359 and forms the core of her passion in Diaspora interests.

When not writing or studying, Genevieve is heavily involved in Advocacy especially for children's mental health.

Genevieve is an administrator, but her hobbies include designing her own clothing and jewellery, research, and searching for antiques and books.

Contact Information: trinineconsultancy@gmail.com

Made in the USA
Columbia, SC
03 November 2024

45188500R00059